ALPHA AND OMEGA

Kate and Humphrey's Big Adventure

by Rebecca McCarthy

ISBN 978-0-545-21460-5

© 2010 Alpha & Omega Productions, LLC. All Rights Reserved.
Published by Scholastic Inc.
SCHOLASTIC and associated logos are trademarks and/or registered trademarks of Scholastic Inc.

12 11 10 9 8 7 6 5 4 3 2 1   10 11 12 13 14 15/0

Printed in the U.S.A.   40
First printing, September 2010

Scholastic Inc.

New York   Toronto   London   Auckland
Sydney   Mexico City   New Delhi   Hong Kong

Dear Readers,

My name is Christina Ricci and I play Lilly in *Alpha and Omega*. Lilly was a very fun part to play, especially because she was a wolf! Wolves are really amazing animals, and I'm glad you watched the movie to learn more about them. This book is packed with lots of other fun facts about wolves.

Sadly, lots of wolves around the world are in trouble right now. They are having trouble finding food, water, and safe places to live. You can help them out by asking your teacher or librarian about volunteering in your area. There are lots of groups that aid wildlife, and I'm sure your local group would love the extra help—no matter how old you are! Animals like Lilly and Garth will be thanking you!

I hope you enjoy this great story and all the fun wolf facts based on the movie!

Your friend,

Christina

Christina

KATE: Hi, I'm Kate! I'm a strong, responsible Alpha wolf. This is Humphrey! He's a silly and playful Omega wolf.

HUMPHREY: Excuse me, *ahem*, you forgot charming, valiant, and dashingly handsome.

KATE: I'm going to tell you the story of how we united the eastern pack wolves and the western pack wolves. It's an exciting adventure story.

HUMPHREY: No, it's the story of how we fell in luuuuuv and it's a luuuuuv story!

KATE: It all started when my father, Winston, the leader of the western pack, promised Tony, the leader of the eastern pack, that I would marry his son, an Alpha wolf named Garth.

HUMPHREY: . . . Which was a *terrible* idea. Barf was all wrong for you. Good-looking, but his howl sounded like a coyote's claws on a chalkboard.

KATE: I knew I needed to marry Garth in order to unite the packs, so I agreed. But . . .

HUMPHREY: . . . that first date didn't go so well, did it? A few minutes into the moonlight howl, Kate ditched Garth to come meet me by the lake.

KATE: I did not ditch Garth! I just . . . needed some water! And I didn't know you'd be there!

HUMPHREY: Riiiiiight . . . .

KATE: Anyway, at the lake at the bottom of the hill, I suddenly felt dizzy. Everything faded to black, and then both Humphrey and I fell into a deep sleep.

HUMPHREY: But just before falling asleep, Kate told me I was cute!

KATE: Did not!

HUMPHREY: Did, too—don't deny it, Kate. Now tell the story, exactly as it happened. What comes next?

KATE: (growls) . . .

KATE: When we woke up, human park rangers released us into Sawtooth National Wilderness in Idaho, which is thousands of miles away from our home!

HUMPHREY: Yeah, we're from Canada, eh? Home of hockey, moose, thick bacon, and maple syrup!

KATE: We met two new friends—a duck named Paddy and a goose named Marcel. They were playing golf. Humphrey didn't get along too well with Marcel at first. Remember?

HUMPHREY: Yes, I remember. I was hoping to forget, but thanks. Thanks for including this bit in the story.

KATE: Hey—I'm just telling the story *exactly* as it happened. . . .

KATE: Paddy and Marcel showed us a camper that belonged to a pair of humans. Since the humans would be driving up to Jasper Park, Canada, soon, we sneaked into the back of their camper to get a free ride.

HUMPHREY: But before getting into the camper, we shared a lovely dance together, and that's when Kate really started to fall for me.

KATE: What? No, *you* started to fall for *me*.

HUMPHREY: No, *you* . . .

KATE: The trip was going well, until the camper arrived at a rest stop. Humphrey stepped outside for a moment, and of course he got distracted by a chubby boy with a cupcake, and then . . .

HUMPHREY: . . . then they started shooting at me! Man, humans do *not* like to share their cupcakes!

KATE: So we ran away into the forest to safety. I was . . . a little angry with Humphrey.

HUMPHREY: Aw, come on! How can you be mad at this face? I'm so cute!

KATE: Then it started to rain. The ground was so slippery that I slid down a ravine, and then . . .

HUMPHREY: . . . and then you remember what I did next?

KATE: What?

HUMPHREY: I rescued you!

KATE: Marcel and Paddy flew in to tell us there was a train that could get us home, and we could catch it on the other side of the mountain. So we began to climb.

HUMPHREY: No, wait—I rescued her. I was a hero!

KATE: Well, we wouldn't have even been in that mess in the first place if it wasn't for you! How could you be so irresponsible?

HUMPHREY: I'm an Omega. "Irresponsible" is my middle name.

KATE: Climbing the mountain was tough because there was snow on the ground.

HUMPHREY: Climbing the mountain was fun because there was snow on the ground!

KATE: Humphrey found a bear cub and started to play with it, which, I have to admit, was very cute.

HUMPHREY: See that? You did think I was cute! You admit it!

KATE: No, I thought the baby bear was cute . . . and I thought the mama bear behind you was not as cute!

KATE: That mama bear started chasing Humphrey, and then more bears came out from behind the trees and started chasing us both! We ran away as fast as we could, and only stopped when we found ourselves at the edge of a cliff. We thought we were done for!

HUMPHREY: Never fear, Humphrey's here! There was a log hanging over the edge of the cliff, so Kate and I hopped on board. We rode that log down the snow-covered mountain, sped up toward a ramp at the end of the embankment . . .

KATE: . . . and then soared through the air all the way to the Canadian Express!

HUMPHREY: We were a great team!

KATE: Right—you get us into trouble and I get us out of it.

HUMPHREY: Whatever works!

KATE: Humphrey and I arrived home just in time. A war was about to break out between the packs! I said I would marry Garth and unite the packs, and this seemed to make everyone very happy.

HUMPHREY: Well, *almost* everyone.

KATE: Lilly helped me get ready for the wedding. She looked so sad and I wondered why.

HUMPHREY: Uh, hello-o? Because you were about to marry her dreamboat, duh! Garth and Lilly spent a lot of time together while Kate and I were gone on our date.

KATE: It wasn't a date.

HUMPHREY: Was, too. There was dinner, there was dancing, we were chased by angry bears—it was a perfect date!

KATE: During the wedding ceremony, as I was about to say, "I
do," I suddenly backed away and realized I couldn't do it.

HUMPHREY: Why, Kate? Why couldn't you do it? Tell everyone why!

KATE: Because I was in love with . . .

HUMPHREY: Meeeeeee!!!!

KATE: (sigh) And Garth was in love with Lilly.

KATE: Just as I feared, Tony did not accept that his Alpha son wanted to marry Lilly—an Omega. In a fit of anger, he declared war on our pack. But just as they were about to attack . . .

HUMPHREY: . . .Stampede!!!

KATE: I sprang into action, and Humphrey joined me. We jumped on a log and rode it toward the stampeding caribou.

HUMPHREY: Roll left! Roll right! Ha, ha—that was fun!

KATE: We landed ahead of the herd, grabbed Tony and Winston, and we all hid behind the log for protection while the caribou ran past!

HUMPHREY: I'll say it again—we make a great team!

KATE: But one of the caribou knocked me out of my hiding place as he ran by us.

HUMPHREY: That was the worst part of the whole date.

KATE: Adventure. That was the worst part of the whole adventure.

HUMPHREY: Date. That was the worst part of the whole date. I thought Kate was badly hurt. After the stampede, she lay on the ground, not moving. I started howling sadly. The other wolves joined in, one by one. Soon, all the wolves in both packs were howling together, all for poor Kate.

KATE: But then I woke up! It takes more than a little stampeding caribou to get me down! My parents were so happy to see that I was okay, that they consented to my marriage to Humphrey, and Lilly's marriage to Garth.

HUMPHREY: Yep—the Alphas and Omegas found love, the eastern and western wolf packs united, and we all lived happily ever after!

KATE: What a great adventure story!

HUMPHREY: You mean, what a great luuuuuv story!

KATE: Oh, brother . . .

HUMPHREY: Hee, hee!

There was a time in our history when hunters had killed nearly all the wolves in America. In 1973, when the Endangered Species Act began protecting gray wolves, there were fewer than 400 wolves in the U.S.

Park Rangers then brought some wolves down to America from Canada and helped them build new homes here. Today, there are more than 3,000 wolves in America!

"Stop the Insanity!
Make Love, Not War!"

Pups begin wrestling for dominance right away. They try to get to the food first and block each other out with their bodies as a way of figuring out who are going to be the Alphas and who are going to be the Omegas.

"That little guy—he's an Omega."

Once the pups are born, the mother feeds them milk for a short time, but soon they start eating the same food as the adults.

"Why are they looking at us so hungrily?"

"Je ne sais quoi. You wolves—you have never seen a golfer before?"

A wolf pack can only raise one litter at a time. Each member of the pack helps to clean out the den to prepare for the arrival of the pups. They also protect the den from predators, and bring back food from hunts for the mother to eat.

"Kate, you take Hutch and Can-Do out to find some food. Lilly, Garth, you take some Betas out with you to mark our territory and make sure no one crosses our borders. Humphrey, you take out this smelly garbage."

Did you know that wolves do not really howl at the moon? It's an old wives' tale! They may howl to each other while the moon is shining, but they are not howling *at* the moon.

"Really? Aw, come on—I was just getting the hang of it!"

Art Wolfe/Stone/Getty Images

Another reason wolves howl is to keep neighboring packs away. If an intruder steps onto a wolf pack's territory, the Alpha male may howl at him in a low voice until he leaves.

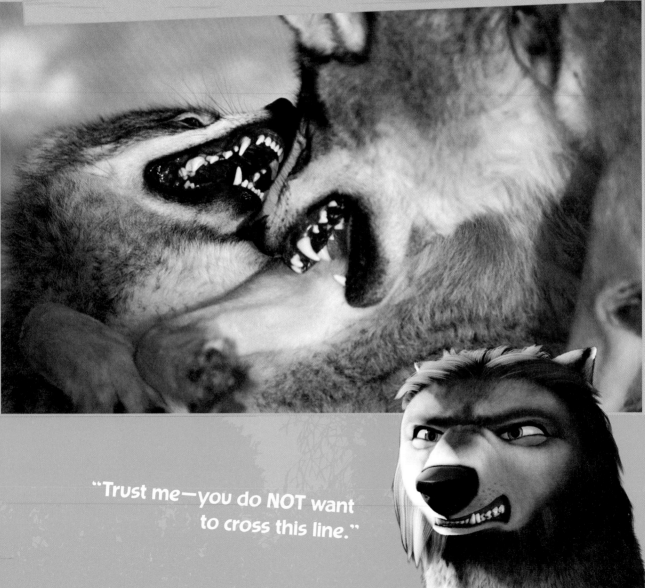

Terje Rakke/Riser/Getty Images

"Trust me—you do NOT want to cross this line."

Wolves can bark, whine, growl, whimper, and, of course, howl. Because wolves wander far and wide to find food, they often become separated from one another. Howling is a way for a wolf to call over great distances to his pack. A wolf howls, his pack answers him with a howl, and he can then find his way home to them.

"A pack that howls together, stays together."

If a wolf crosses the border into another pack's territory, a fight may break out. They may have a howling contest, they may wrestle until one wolf is pinned to the ground, or they may just fight it out with claws and fangs. The winning pack takes over the land.

"What's ours is ours, and what's yours is ours, get it?"

Wolves are territorial creatures, which means they like to have a piece of land all their own. They roam their territory and mark the borders of their land, so that other wolves know not to intrude.

"Yeah! Stay off our turf!"

A wolf den is a small, dark place underground with a tunnel leading to it. The Alpha female tries to choose a place for her den that has water nearby. Some dens are used year after year, but sometimes, a new den has to be dug by the mother.

"You're going to love this next den, Mr. and Mrs. Wolf. Formerly occupied by a fox, it's a bit of a fixer-upper, but you can't beat the location. There are spectacular mountain views, it's walking distance to the lake, and there's a five-star Alpha school just up the road!"

Wolves are carnivores, or meat eaters. They like elk, moose, deer, and caribou. When meat is scarce, wolves will eat other foods such as berries, grasshoppers, and even earthworms.

Media Bakery

"Plants are tasty!"

"Go vegan!"

Alpha wolves also decide when and where to hunt, when the pack is going to travel and to where, and also when the pack is going to attack an enemy pack of wolves.

Jean Apul Ferrero/Ardea

"Dominance has its privileges!"

Alpha wolves are often the only ones who mate and have pups. They also get to eat first, and make sure their young pups eat enough before the older wolves start feeding.

"Aw, go ahead, little fellas."

The Omegas are the lowest ranking wolves in the pack. They eat last, and relieve tension in the group when things go wrong, such as a bad hunt. Omega is the last letter in the Greek alphabet.

"Hey, um, are you gonna eat all that? Because if you're not I'd be happy to help out. Hey, hey, guys—throw me a bone? Does anyone not like theirs? I'll be happy to trade these berries for some of that meat."

There is a group of young adults below the Alpha male and female called the Beta wolves. They help with hunting, support the Alphas, and make sure all the other wolves listen to the Alphas' orders. Beta is the second letter in the Greek alphabet.

"We Alphas wouldn't be able to lead without a strong team of Betas to support us."

"Yeah!"

"What she said!"

Each member of the wolf pack has a rank and an important job to do. The Alpha male and Alpha female are the dominant members of the pack and have the most experience in hunting, defending territory, creating a den, traveling, and other activities. Alpha is the first letter of the Greek alphabet.

John Pitcher/AGE Fotostock

"In Alpha school, they taught us all about pack leadership, responsibility, honor, courage, and commitment!"

"In Omega school, they taught us how to make spit balls."

When the pups are old enough to leave home, usually by age three, they go out in search of a mate and start new packs of their own.

"Someday my prince will come . . ."

Packs are usually made up of six or seven wolves, although some may be larger. The wolf pack family is made up of the mama and papa wolf, and their offspring.

The more wolves in a pack, the easier it is to defend territory from enemies.

"Ow, you're standing on my tail. Oooow!"

"They don't mess with us cuz we're so tough!"

"Yeah, when Scar and Claw come around, we give 'em the ol' one-two!"

While a mother wolf nurses her young pups, the other wolves bring food for her.

"I'll have four cheeseburgers, two carne asada tacos, three slices of pepperoni pizza, a bucket of extra crispy fried chicken . . ."

"You want fries with that?"

Pack living is much better for wolves than living alone. The more adults there are, the easier it is to hunt for food.

"I would never lead a hunt without my team!"

Usually, the Alpha male is in charge of the entire pack. But during the mating season, the Alpha female takes over. She is in charge of all the wolves, from the adults to the pups — even the Alpha male!

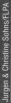

"You were saying?"

"Um, yes, dear. I mean, no, dear. I mean, whatever you say, dear!"

A wolf pack is a group of wolves that live together, very much like a human family. They travel, hunt, howl, raise pups, and play together.

"And I'm the Alpha male! The head honcho! The big kahuna!"

ALPHA AND OMEGA

All About Wolves

by Rebecca McCarthy

ISBN 978-0-545-21460-5

© 2010 Alpha & Omega Productions, LLC. All Rights Reserved.

Back cover photo: Geoffrey Kuchera/Shutterstock

Published by Scholastic Inc.

SCHOLASTIC and associated logos are trademarks and/or registered trademarks of Scholastic Inc.

12 11 10 9 8 7 6 5 4 3 2 1   10 11 12 13 14 15/0

Printed in the U.S.A.   40

First printing, September 2010

Scholastic Inc.

**New York   Toronto   London   Auckland
Sydney   Mexico City   New Delhi   Hong Kong**